JOËL MALM

GUIDED
by
THUNDER

A TALE OF **ADVENTURE**
AND **REDISCOVERY**
IN A **FOREIGN LAND**

Guided by Thunder: A Tale of Adventure and Rediscovery in a Foreign Land
by Joël Malm

Copyright © 2020 by Joël Malm

joelmalm.com

ISBN 978-0-9985085-6-6

Map copyright © 2020 Joël Malm
Map design by Chaim Holtjer

Cover design and interior layout by Five J's Design
Author photograph by Brad Roberts

GUIDED
by
THUNDER

A TALE OF **ADVENTURE**
AND **REDISCOVERY**
IN A **FOREIGN LAND**

JOËL MALM

MGPRESS

NOTE TO THE READER

The first time I ever climbed a major mountain, our team got into a precarious situation with weather and injuries.

We were rescued by a Norwegian named Torgrim (which means Thor's helmet).

The name of my hero in this book is in honor of that Nordic Guardian Angel.

1

EVERETT ANDERSON SAT ON THE BALCONY
overlooking the giant Plaza de Armas — the central square of
Cusco, Peru. The plaza was flanked on all sides by 500-year-
old Spanish buildings with long loggias and two giant cathe-
drals on the perimeter. In the center was a fountain, sitting
areas, and perfectly manicured gardens of flowers and freshly
cut grass. A patch of grey clouds was forming around a snow
covered mountain peak at the far end of the valley. Thunder
rumbled in the distance.

He still couldn't quite believe he was deep in the Andes Mountains. His first time south of the equator. His first time in South America. On a whim, he had purchased the ticket just a week earlier. It all felt a bit surreal. He took a sip of his dark, chalky coffee and tried to calm down while soaking it all in.

"*Hallo*, lost man! What are you doing in Peru?" a voice thundered next to him. Everett turned to see a giant man with long blonde hair in a braid, forcefully set down two beer steins and sit on the edge of the table. The giant slid one of the beers toward Everett, unconcerned about the foam that sloshed across the table.

Everett wasn't really interested in chatting, but something about the man's Nordic accent and size seemed to demand a response. "Uh. Going to Machu Picchu. You?"

"When do you start your hike?"

"Uhm. Well, I'm not hiking. I've got a tour lined up. I'm taking the train."

"Ha! The train?" He chugged his beer and slammed the stein back down on the table. "Why are you not hiking?"

The question and the man's tone made Everett feel small. He did his best to project confidence. "I guess I didn't realize hiking was an option." *And I've never hiked a day in my life,* he thought. "And, I'm not that adventurous."

The giant man raised his eyebrows. "Then why Machu Picchu? That is adventure."

Normally, Everett would have been more annoyed by the conversation. The intrusive questions reminded him of his soon-to-be-ex-wife. But there was something energizing about sitting next to this giant man who resembled Thor, the Norse god of thunder. "I didn't really see it as an adventure, I guess. I think it's more of a last hurrah, before... I don't know."

"Before what?"

"It's complicated."

"Before what?"

Everett shifted in his chair, turning to face his inquisitor. "Well, do you want to know the whole story?"

"Did I buy you that beer so we could sit in silence?" He grinned.

Everett took a deep breath. "Well, the global pandemic last year really messed up my life. I lost my job, my wife, my dream house, and my..." His voice trailed off as he looked out the window at the snow covered mountain at the end of the valley.

"Your what?"

Everett couldn't bring himself to look at the giant man. "I guess I lost my sense of direction."

"Pfft! The pandemic made you lose direction? Maybe it just revealed your lack of direction."

Everett felt a rush of heat to his forehead, his jaw tightened. He didn't like where this conversation was going. He held a smile and changed the topic. "I didn't get your name. I'm Everett, by the way." He went to shake his hand, but remembered many people still weren't comfortable shaking hands. So he shifted into a fist, for a fist bump.

But the man wrapped his giant hand around Everett's fist, shaking it. "I am Torgrim."

"Tor-gurm?" he said, pulling his fist out of the man's vice grip.

"No." The man frowned. "Tor. Grim. Torgrim," he said, flexing his biceps and waving his fists high in the air to accent each syllable.

"Ah. Gotcha. Where are you from, Torgrim."

"Norway. And you are American."

"Yes. Could you tell from the accent?"

"No. I can just tell. Why go to Machu Picchu if you don't like adventure and have no direction?"

Geez. Everett thought. *This guy is relentless.* "If you really want to know. I'm about two weeks away from being a single man, again. I've been responsible my whole life. I've played by all the rules. I took out a massive loan to pay for college. Got my degree and went straight to work. I got married. Had kids. Got a mortgage for my dream home. Worked my tail off to pay the bills and provide for my family. I gave that company the best years of my life — worked loads of unpaid overtime — and then, at the first sign of the financial crisis from the pandemic, they decided I was nonessential." He turned his head and stared out over the plaza. His fist clenched tight, partially from anger, but partially because Torgrim had squeezed it so hard he couldn't open it fully again. "And, don't even get me started on my marriage. I guess this is my screw-it-all trip." He turned back to look at Torgrim. "I'm doing what I want for once. I'm gonna be reckless and pay for it later."

Torgrim's eyes narrowed. He gave Everett a piercing look. After a moment he grunted then took another giant chug of his beer.

Everett felt like a fool. He had shared way too much with this random Norwegian. He took a few sips of the beer Torgrim had given him, then signaled at the waiter to request his bill. The waiter brought the bill as the two men sat in silence.

Everett was shuffling through the Peruvian soles in his wallet, trying to distinguish the different bank notes, when

Torgrim spoke up. "Put your money away." He handed a 100 soles bill to the waiter. "Keep the change."

The waiter's face lit up. "Thank you, señor!"

Torgrim stood. "Evelyn, the train is not what you need. You must hike to Machu Picchu." He grabbed a napkin, scribbled something on it, then dropped it in front of Everett. "Buy these items and meet me at the address on that napkin tomorrow at 5:00 a.m." He turned and walked away, giving the waiter a high five as he stepped out the door of the restaurant.

Everett glanced at the napkin. It was a list of items for hiking. He turned to protest. "Wait. I can't hike. I —" But Torgrim was gone. He looked back at the napkin and mumbled to himself. "I can't hike…and I'm sure not going to do it with some giant Norwegian I just met. And did he just call me Evelyn?"

He put his money away, thanked the waiter, then walked toward his hotel through the main plaza. He couldn't shake the image of the giant man inviting him to hike. *What made him think I could do a hike?* He thought about the strange impulse of courage — or possibly recklessness — that had led him to come to Peru. The entire experience, from buying the ticket to actually boarding the flight to somewhere unknown, had been new and foreign, and, well, exciting. Which is exactly what he had hoped for. He needed a new start. Clearly what he had been doing wasn't working. His life was a mess. He was starting over.

He stood staring at the giant fountain in the middle of the square. He really was determined to start over. Should he start by doing the opposite of his natural instinct and see what happened? He shook the thought from his head as he scanned the plaza, hoping to see Torgrim's bright blonde hair towering above the small crowd. The sun was setting and businesses were beginning to turn on their outside lights. One business in particular stood out. The illuminated sign said, "Outdoors gears." Everett pulled the crumpled napkin out of his pocket and looked at it. *Am I crazy? I've never hiked anywhere in my life.* He walked across the plaza toward the store. A smiling Peruvian man greeted him. "Buenas tardes, señor. What can I help you find?"

Everett glanced to his left and then his right, unsure why he felt so embarrassed. "Uhm, do you sell these items." He handed the smiling man the crumpled napkin.

The man glanced at it. "Of course."

"Could I take a look at them?"

"Sure. Come in. Where are you going?"

"Uhm. Well, I'm thinking of hiking to Machu Picchu."

The Peruvian man's eyes widened. "I hope you already have the other things you need. This list is not enough for the hike."

"Well, the guy..." He realized how strange this was going to sound if he had to explain it all. "I mean, the guide, he said this was all I need."

"Pfft! Ay yay yay. He must be a horrible guide. You need more than this friend. This is a very difficult hike. And you are a *gringo*. Listen, I will get you everything you need." He crumpled up the napkin and threw it into a pink, plastic garbage bin in the corner.

Thirty minutes and $600 later, Everett emerged from the store with a giant backpack filled with all sorts of gear. He felt dazed and confused. *Am I really doing this?* He marched back to his hotel, doing his best to shift the pack into a comfortable position. By the time he got there he was exhausted. The bag was so heavy. *There's no way I can do this hike. I can't even make it to my hotel.* Panic rushed over him as he opened the door to his hotel room. *What am I doing?*

He lay on his bed, trying to catch his breath from the 11,000 foot altitude. He thought about all that had happened in the last two hours. The strange Norwegian. The spending spree, buying gear he had never heard of in his life. He laughed at himself. "This is insane."

He needed to pack and prepare, but he closed his eyes for a moment and instantly fell asleep.

JOËL MALM

JOËL MALM

2

EVERETT AWOKE IN A PANIC. HE ROLLED
over and grabbed his iPhone. *4:45 a.m.!* He hadn't intended to
fall asleep. He hadn't showered or packed anything other than
what he had just bought in the backpack. Now he had fifteen
minutes to get to the meeting point. His heart sank, followed
by a sense of relief. This was the excuse he needed. He had no
business hiking to Machu Picchu anyway. Last night was a
strange impulse. Who did he think he was? Maybe the outdoor store would let him return the gear.

He lay back on the bed, but instantly a jolt of adrenaline shot through his body. He knew he had to do this. He looked at his phone again. *4:49 a.m.* He hoisted the pack onto his back and headed out the door.

The dark streets of Cuzco were nearly empty. A gentle glow from the soon-rising sun hovered over the mountains around the city. Everett felt tired and exhilarated all at the same time. It was 5:01 a.m. and he still had at least two blocks to go. Looking down the cobblestone street he could make out Torgrim's bright blonde hair as he stepped out of a building and walked toward a white Land Cruiser.

Everett started running. He watched as Torgrim jumped on top of the Land Cruiser, seemingly in one leap and strapped down his backpack. Everett ran up to the Land Cruiser. "Torgrim, I'm here." His lungs were aching from the lack of oxygen in the 11,000 foot altitude. "Sorry I'm late. I...well, I wasn't even sure I was going to do this."

Torgrim stood up straight on the roof rack, looking down on Everett. The sun was rising behind him, creating an orange glow around his chiseled frame. Everett couldn't help but laugh at the scene, it looked like Thor surveying his kingdom and subjects.

"Evelyn, what in God's name did you bring on your back?" He jumped off the Land Cruiser and landed on his feet next to Everett. The ground shook and a chunk of plaster fell off the wall on the building next to them.

"Well, the man at the outdoor st —"

Torgrim ripped the bag off Everett's back, unzipped it, and started digging through it. "You will kill yourself carrying all this." He pulled out all the new gear, with tags still on it, and threw it onto the sidewalk. A small pile was forming.

"Hey! What if I need that?"

"You won't."

"But what if I do?"

"You will improvise. Get in the truck."

Everett stood there, stunned, watching all his brand new gear being thrown onto the sidewalk. Torgrim looked up and gave him a fierce stare. Everett opened the Land Cruiser door and slipped into the passenger seat. He watched as the giant man zipped the bag back up, threw the pack over his shoulder, and in one motion vaulted himself off the back tire and back onto the roof rack. The car shook violently. Everett looked at the back of the Land Cruiser. It was filled with crates and trunks. *Does he live in here?* The car shook again as Torgrim leapt off the roof rack and hopped into the driver's seat. The engine surged to life. "Buckle up." He grunted as they began driving away.

"Wait, what about all my gear?" He looked in the rearview mirror as they drove away from the pile on the street. "You just left it on the sidewalk."

"You don't need it. Buckle up."

"But, I just bought all that stuff. It's new. And it was expensive."

"Then someone will be very happy to find it. You will thank me later. Buckle up."

Everett felt adrenaline surge into his chest. "Stop! Stop now!"

Torgrim slammed on the brakes and Everett flew into the dashboard. It knocked the breath out of him. He felt a sharp pain in his shoulder from hitting the hard surface.

Torgrim stared at him for a moment. Then motioned with his head, his braided ponytail flipping over his shoulder and onto his chest. "Go. Get your stuff. Take the train to Machu Picchu."

Everett gave him an incredulous look. "But…"

"Go." Torgrim motioned with his hand.

"Look, I...I think I want to do this. But the way you're talking to me... I'm a grown man, not some boy you can treat like —"

"Like your company treated you when they fired you for being nonessential?"

Everett was furious. "Who do you think you are?" He slammed his hand on the seat, causing a jolt of pain through his shoulder. He raised his voice. "Look, I really don't know what I'm doing here. And I told you all that personal stuff because you asked. Now you're using it against me!"

Torgrim smiled. "Aha! There *is* fire in you. I like the fire Evy. Keep the fire. And trust me, you don't need all that stuff." He pulled his foot off the brake and they started rolling forward again. "People will sell you many things they say you can't live without. They will scare you, saying you must have it. But light loads make happy travelers. All you need is courage. Face the unknown, empty-handed and alone. Now, buckle up... Please." He offered a faint smile.

Everett was still pressed up against the dashboard, rubbing his shoulder. He looked back and saw two boys running off with his gear in their arms. He sighed, then leaned back into the seat and pulled the strap across his chest. His head was aching and he felt dazed as the vehicle surged forward and they rumbled through the empty cobblestone streets of Cuzco.

They drove in silence for about two hours over a winding asphalt road. Everett fell in and out of sleep. The paved road ended and they began bumping down a dirt road alongside a rushing river. He looked at the giant snowcapped peaks surrounding them. "Are we going to be hiking through that snow?" he asked.

"Maybe. Sometimes snow. Sometimes brutal heat."

Everett sighed. "That was some good gear you threw out back there."

"Yes. But too much. You must prioritize. Choose what to take and what to leave behind. On the trail and in life."

Everett made a hissing sound. "You sound like my ex-wife, or soon-to-be-ex-wife. Always complaining that my priorities were out of line. 'You work too much. You think buying one more *thing* is going to make you happy. You never have time for the kids.'"

Torgrim looked at him with the same piercing look he had seen the day before at the cafe. "Was she right?"

Everett swallowed, trying to clear the dust from his throat.

He looked out the window. "I don't know. Maybe. I was trying to make a good life for them…and me. I wanted to give them all the things I didn't have growing up. That's why I worked so much. I bought all that stuff because I worked hard and I, they, deserved it."

"Fortjent," Torgrim mumbled and laughed to himself.

"What does that mean?"

"Everly, you can't carry everything. You only have so much time, money, and energy. You must prioritize."

"It's Everett," he mumbled. "And prioritizing must be easy for someone who lives out of his Land Cruiser."

Torgrim slammed on the brakes, skidding the truck to a halt in a dust cloud. "Everyone has a backpack in life. You, me, everyone. We all fill our life backpack with things we think we need. But most realize too late that it was filled with the wrong things." They drove in silence for a few more minutes before Torgrim parked next to a small adobe hut. "We start here."

He jumped on top of the car, put both backpacks over his shoulders, then hopped back down. The ground shook and a layer of dust fell off the vehicle.

"So, what time do you think we'll get back?" Everett asked.

"Evening."

"Really? That's late." He looked at his watch. It was 8:00 a.m. "How far is Machu Picchu from here?"

"Fifty kilometers."

"What?" He didn't know kilometers well, but he knew that was no day, or two-day, hike. "How are we gonna hike that far?"

"One step at a time. Four days."

"Four days?"

Torgrim laughed, dropping Everett's pack at his feet. "What did you think this hike was, Ebony, a walk through Central Park?" He slapped him on the back.

Everett hoisted his backpack onto his shoulders and was shocked at just how light it was now. It was almost a comforting weight, like something was wrapped around him — a burden that felt manageable. Maybe he could do four days after all...

JOËL MALM

3

3

THEY WALKED ALONG A CHURNING GREEN
river filled with giant boulders. The whitewater rapids and
waves they created looked treacherous. The river snaked its
way through the valley, flanked by a long ridge of towering,
snowcapped mountains.

"We cross there." Torgrim pointed.

Everett felt a jolt of panic as he looked at the narrow
rope bridge that hung over the river. The bridge extended

from some sort of ancient Inca watchtower perched on a cliff overlooking the rapids. There was only enough room for one person at a time to cross. As they approached it, he noticed several planks were missing at random places in the bridge. "Is that safe?"

Torgrim laughed. "Probably."

"It seems dangerous."

"Yes. Life is danger. You cannot avoid it. You go first. I will follow."

"Uhm. You outweigh me by about one hundred pounds." He looked at Torgrim's giant, muscular frame. "You go first. I'm terrified of heights."

"No. Go!" Torgrim roared, snapping his finger as he pointed ahead. "I will be behind you."

Everett was so shaken by the thunderous voice that he complied. But as he took the first step onto the rickety structure his body froze. He looked down at the churning water and began to feel dizzy. His hands squeezed the moldy ropes and his breathing nearly stopped. He turned back to run away, but slammed into Torgrim. It felt like hitting a brick wall. He shook off the shock. "I can't do this. Really, I have a major fear of heights. I don't want to die."

Torgrim laughed. "You died a long time ago, Eggeret." He pulled Everett off the bridge, then placed one hand on each shoulder and squared off with him, looking him straight in the eyes. "There will always be fear. Good fear keeps you out of trouble. But bad fear keeps you from living."

"Living? I might die!" Everett looked over his shoulder at the roaring rapids below.

"You must conquer your fear. Face what you fear in small doses. Build immunity to fear. Take one step. Survive. Another step. Survive. This is how you really live! Now cross!" There was a fierce determination in Torgrim's eyes.

Everett took a deep breath, then turned and began walking slowly. He took one step onto the bridge and froze.

"Breathe and move ahead," Torgrim said in a surprisingly gentle tone.

Everett took another step, then another. He started moving at a consistent pace, but as he did the bridge began to sway and shake. He dropped to one knee, adrenaline pulsing through his chest. At that moment, Torgrim stepped onto the bridge, making it bounce even more. Everett wanted to scream, but he didn't have any breath to do it.

Torgrim shouted over the roaring river. "Pick a point ahead. Lock your eyes on it. Go toward it."

Everett took a deep breath, locked his eyes onto a wooden sign at the end of the bridge that said *PELIGRO* in bright yellow letters, and stood. He began walking forward, doing his best to maintain his balance with the bridge shaking up and down and left and right. Little by little he found his pace and balance. He didn't look down. He just walked ahead as confidently as he could. "One step at a time," he whispered to himself.

When he took the last step off the bridge and onto solid ground he dropped to his knees and collapsed in a patch of lush green grass. Behind him, Torgrim began clapping as he walked confidently across the bridge. "Courage! Now you are living."

"Living? Ha!" Everett pointed back at the bridge. "That was terrifying!"

"Living takes courage. You must take risks. Your journey has now begun. You have passed the first waypoint — courage. Well done, Everett."

Everett looked up. "Hey, that's the first time you've called me by my real name."

"That's the first time you've lived up to it." Torgrim grinned, then marched ahead.

Everett hopped up and ran to catch him. "Man, that was crazy back there." Everett shook his head, feeling a sense of accomplishment and calm overcome him. "I felt…like…that was the scariest and most exciting thing I think I've ever done. I'm in Peru, hiking to Machu Picchu, walking over an ancient Inca rope bridge."

Torgrim laughed. "I told you, you died a long time ago. You are coming back to life now. And that bridge was made last year."

They walked in silence for a few minutes, listening to the roar of the river below that bounced off the walls of the surrounding mountains.

"What did you mean when you said I died a long time ago?" Everett asked.

"You have been afraid to really live. Fear makes your world small. It makes you only focus on avoiding loss. Try to avoid all loss and you will become weak and die inside. Life doesn't get easier. You must get stronger."

"I don't feel like I'm afraid of living."

"Fear has many faces." He stopped and smiled, pointing his finger down the valley. "A condor."

Everett looked ahead and saw a giant bald-headed bird soaring through the valley, backdropped by a snowcapped peak. He pulled out his phone to take a picture. Torgrim grunted, "No." He slapped Everett's hand so hard that the phone flew out of his hand and bounced down to the churning river below. "My phone! What the —? That's an expensive phone!"

"You won't need it. No signal. Now you can focus and be present."

Torgrim marched ahead, but Everett stood staring at the spot in the roaring river where his phone had disappeared into the water. Torgrim was now far down the trail, so Everett had to run to catch up. He was irritated and angry. He managed to catch back up to Torgrim and found a steady pace behind him. At least he had loss insurance on the phone. He'd get a new one. But he was tempted to turn back. They were still close to where they started. Was losing his phone worth giving up on whatever this was? He took a deep breath and decided he'd better let it go if he wanted to keep a good relationship with this borderline insane man.

He found a good pace behind Torgrim and began to calm down. "What do you mean fear has many faces?"

"Anxiety, worry, indecision, checking out. All fear. Everyone is afraid in some way."

"How do you know everyone is afraid?"

"We all have a deer, wolf, and walrus inside us. The deer wants security. The wolf wants connection with a pack. And the walrus wants control."

"Hold on," Everett said. "I mean, I can see that. I want to be safe. To have relationships. And I want to have some amount of control. But what does that have to do with fear?"

"Everyone is afraid of not getting security, connection, or control. We believe money, a job, power, or sex will bring them. They don't. All those things can be taken away. Deep down, we know this. So we are afraid. Everywhere. Everyone. Fear is contagious. Fortunately, so is courage."

The wind was beginning to pick up as the path curved onto a dry plateau with patches of scrub brush. They stopped at a cliff overlooking a lush green valley with a river running through it. Stone crop terraces covered the sides of all the mountains along the river. A group of stone buildings sat at the base of the terraces. "Are those Inca ruins?" he asked.

"Yes. This is the Sacred Valley of the Incas. Those are the ruins of Llaqtapata."

"That's a weird name." He tried to say it, but couldn't.

"Yahkta-pahta," Torgrim annunciated as he dug into his bag and handed Everett a sandwich and an apple. "Lunch."

They both dropped their bags and sat down on a patch of dry, brown grass overlooking the valley. A dry breeze was blowing in their faces.

"Why is it called the Sacred Valley?"

"It was a source of life for the Inca. The river provided for crops. The valley connected them with the Amazon jungle just over those mountains. The climate is mild down there. It's a safe place. Humans always give sacred status to anything that gives security, connection, and control. We know we need a Higher Power to provide for us."

They finished their lunch, then followed the trail along the edge of the cliff until they came to the restored ruins of another Inca structure. They poked their heads inside for a moment and then began descending into a series of switchbacks. The downhill was steep and Everett felt like he had to run to keep from slipping on the dirt.

The trail leveled off at the bottom of the valley. Another river ran to their right. Everett did his best to keep pace with his giant guide's long stride. "So, what is it you do exactly?" he asked.

"I find lost cities."

"Seriously? Are you some sort of archeologist?"

"Mmm." He stopped abruptly. Everett was hiking so close that he slammed into Torgrim's backpack. "That's our campsite up there." Torgrim pointed.

"Way up there?"

"Yes." Torgrim continued walking. They crossed a bridge and went through a sparsely populated village. A group of kids playing soccer stopped their game the moment they saw Torgrim. "Gigante!" shouted one of the kids. Torgrim smiled and waved. They all ran toward him giggling and whispering as they approached.

Torgrim dropped his bag and motioned for one of the kids to kick their soccer ball to him. "Get in there. Let's show them how to play."

Everett reluctantly dropped his bag and ran onto the field. The kids easily beat them in their pickup game. It was clear Everett actually tried while Torgrim took it easy. When the game ended they shook hands with all the kids, loaded up their bags, then continued their hike.

An hour later they arrived at a clearing of soft carpet grass surrounded by thick greenery. A small stream ran next to the campsite. Torgrim pulled a tent from his backpack and set it up with a few flicks of his wrist.

Everett started digging through his bag. "Hey, you threw out my tent!"

"You don't need it. We will share."

"That tent is barely big enough for you. We can't both fit in there."

"Nonsense. I sleep on my side. Plenty of room."

Torgrim prepared them a meal on a small gas canister stove he had in his pack and they sat in the dark, eating. There was no moon and no light pollution, so a sky full of stars glimmered above them.

"This food is surprisingly filling."

"Good. Now for pure water. Pull out your filter."

Everett flipped on his headlamp and reached into his pack. "Glad you left this." He pulled out a canister with a pump lever on it.

"I left everything you need. We filter each night. Our next day depends on it."

They pumped the water from a small brook that ran next to their campsite. Their headlamps illuminated the small stream. "The water looks so clear it seems like you could almost drink it straight from the creek."

"No. One small impurity can cause serious problems. Always filter out the bad each night. On the trail and in life."

"On the trail and in life. You say that a lot."

"Yes. So you do not miss the connection. Life, the trail — the same.

They filled their water containers, cleaned the few dishes, then climbed into their tent. Torgrim went straight to sleep.

Everett lay staring at the tent ceiling, listening to the snoring giant next to him. He thought about the events of the day. He thought about how he was supposed to have already visited Machu Picchu by train. But instead, he had just completed the first of four days of hiking to Machu Picchu with some sort of Nordic Zen-Master. *What on earth am I doing on this journey?*

4

"WAKE UP. TOUGH DAY AHEAD. WE MUST AT- tack it." Torgrim's voice thundered.

Everett opened his eyes and stretched his neck, trying to relieve the sharp pain he felt in his shoulders. "Torgrim, for the record, you don't sleep on your side. You start there, but I spent most of the night contorting my body to avoid having your knee in my chest or crotch."

"Ha! So you slept well?"

"Uh… No. But, at least I was warm. You generate quite a bit of heat buddy." He slapped the tent wall several times to remove the condensation dripping down the side. "It got pretty cold out there last night."

"Yes. It will get colder as we climb."

Great. Everett crawled out of the tent, just in time for it to collapse behind him as Torgrim dismantled it and began folding and packing it. Everett stretched again, taking in the blue hues on the mountains around them, then shoved his few belongings into the backpack. The sun was peaking over the jagged snowcapped peak to the left, creating a gentle glow on their campsite. Add the sound of the brook flowing next to their campsite and it was a peaceful scene. Except for the bugs. Tiny gnats swarmed around Everett's face as he loaded the last of his gear. He looked down and noticed a small spot of blood on his arm. *Did that gnat just bite me?* He went to scratch it, but Torgrim slapped his hand away.

"Don't scratch. Midges. I call them vampire gnats. Scratch their bite and it only gets worse."

"Man, these bugs really ruin a perfect scene. Isn't that the way it always is?"

"Ignore the bugs."

"But they're everywhere. They are all up in my face and biting my skin. How do you ignore a constant irritation?"

"Focus on where you are going — the goal — and the gnats in the way will be insignificant. On the trail and in life."

"Huh?"

Torgrim hissed and shook his head. "Focus on where you are going and little things that bother you will become insignicant."

"I don't understand. What do you mean? How do you ignore something biting you?"

"Focus. Where you are going, right now?"

"Machu Picchu."

"Focus your mind on that. Then you won't worry about petty, small things that bother you."

"On the trail and in life, right?"

"Ah, you are getting it now. How you approach anything is how you approach everything. It is all connected. The way you do this hike is the way you will do life."

"That seems a little fatalistic."

"No. It's reality. *Uten åpenbaring blir folket tøiesløst.*"

"What does that mean?"

"When you don't know what you really want, you'll wander with no direction. The story of your life. You have been

wandering around. Listening to what others tell you to want."
Torgrim charged out of the campsite and onto the trail. The
sun was up now, illuminating the trail ahead.

Everett ran to catch up. "What do you mean?"

Torgrim stopped and turned, giving his piercing stare.
"What do you really want in your life, Everett? Really, deep
inside."

He thought for a moment. "I guess I want those three
things you talked about yesterday. Security, connection, and
control."

"Exactly. And you think you know how to get that."

"Well, I thought I did. I thought I actually had it. But it's
all crumbling now."

"Yes. Because you looked for it in the wrong place."

"Okay. So, where should I have been looking for it?"

"Look to the greatest man who ever lived. He said if you
want security, connection, and a sense of control — don't seek
those things." He poked Everett in the chest several times as
he enunciated each word. "Seek first the Kingdom of God —
a higher way of thinking — and you will get everything you
want. You must have the right aim."

"The Kingdom of God? Didn't Jesus say that?"

"Ah, you know. But you have not done what you know. You go after small, petty things. Which is why small, petty things threaten you."

They walked in silence through a dense stretch of rainforest.

"I didn't realize you were a religious man."

"Not religion. Harmony. Harmony with what you see and don't see. God's order brings harmony."

Everett took a deep breath, trying to process what Torgrim had just said. They rounded a switchback and a seemingly endless stone staircase stretched ahead of them, leading deep into the tropical foliage.

Everett planted his foot on the first step.

Torgrim pointed ahead. "From here on we will hike on original Inca roads."

They began their ascent of the staircase. Some steps were uneven and narrow, others were wide and deep. Within a few minutes Everett was exhausted and panting hard. "Man, this section is no joke."

"It only gets harder."

"*Geez.* Thanks for the encouragement. You'd think that with so many people wanting to visit Machu Picchu, they'd make a new trail that's a little more accessible."

Torgrim grunted. "Everyone wants a new road. They want it easy. Nothing of value comes easy."

"I get that. But hey, we live in the modern age. We have technology and science to make life easier. We've created tools to deal with all our new problems."

"Pssh! New problems!" Torgrim's voice thundered, scaring a flock of parakeets out of a nearby tree. "There are no new problems. There are only old problems with new faces. All problems are the same old problems."

"Well, sort of, I guess. But life is more complex. We have to develop new answers for our complex problems."

"There are no new answers. There are only old answers. Ancient paths. The old path hasn't been found wanting, it has been found difficult and abandoned. The ancient path is hard. But it makes us stronger. When we reject it we become weak and soft."

In life and on the trail, Everett thought. He remained quiet, mostly because he was trying to preserve his oxygen for the endless steps still in front of him. He thought about his life. As much as he complained about his challenges, he had a pretty good life. And, honestly, he did shy away from anything uncomfortable or challenging. He had been pretty lazy and tended to take the path of least resistance. He never spoke up when his bosses asked him to work weekends that took him away from his family. He didn't confront the bad behavior he was seeing in his sons. He didn't address the growing rift he felt between him and his wife. He was tired. He didn't have the energy. When his wife announced she wanted a divorce, it was a relief in a way — until the reality of what it meant hit him. Everett cleared his throat. "So, what do you mean when you say the ancient path?"

"It's harmony with the order God created. Living by His standards and what He says is of greatest value. A proven path to harmony."

"Harmony. I *could* use a little more of that. So what's the order?"

"Prioritize what is most important. Aim at the right things. Then sacrifice good things for the best things — what is most important."

"Prioritize," Everett mumbled. "There's that word again."

They arrived at a section of the trail that ran along a rushing stream, flowing from a cascading waterfall further up the mountain. Different varieties of orchids and ferns were thriving in the heavily shaded undergrowth of the forest. "This is amazing."

"Aye." Torgrim smiled. "Lunch soon. Then the hardest part to Dead Woman's Pass. The highest point of our hike."

Everett took a deep breath and sighed. "Alright. Bring it on," he said with as much gusto as he could drum up.

"Aha! There's the fire. I like it Everett. Embrace the hard path."

They pushed ahead, step by step, up the giant staircase through the forest. As they climbed to a higher altitude the tropical foliage gave way to scrub brush and a few scrawny trees. With less shade and moisture from the foliage it was getting much warmer. They arrived at a clearing and were greeted by two dusty brown and white llamas munching on a patch of scrub brush.

"Look, up there." Torgrim pointed to a dip between two mountains. "Dead Woman's Pass. No shade on that trail. These clouds are good. Cooler." Torgrim patted both llamas as he walked past them.

Everett could see a steep trail snaking its way along the mountain, all the way to the pass. This was not going to be easy. He walked past the llamas and reached out to pet one, but it turned and bit his hand. Then it rammed its head into him, biting at his arm. Everett let out a yelp and quickly moved away. But the llama kept chasing him across the dusty clearing. Everett ran to hide behind Torgrim, who just laughed and shooed the llama away.

"Nasty but beautiful beasts. Related to camels. They spit too. Here." Torgrim handed him dried sausages, an orange, and some chips.

Everett sat down and devoured the food. He leaned back on a patch of grass, staring up at the thick ceiling of clouds above him. "You said I have to aim at the right things. How do you know what the right things are?"

"Ah, the great challenge of life. Many things to aim at. They change — moving targets. But two never change." He tore a piece of sausage with his teeth and chewed, staring at the mountains around them.

Everett gave an inquisitive look, making a forward stirring motion with his hand. "So what two things don't change?"

Torgrim locked eyes with Everett. "Love God. Love people. In that order."

"Ah. Back to religion."

"Wrong. Harmony. Religion is work, trying to do enough. You've worked hard and look what it got you. Harmony is surrender. Stop trying to provide your own security, connection, and control. Let go of your pride. Humble yourself. Seek what God values and you get it all."

"You mean follow the rules?"

"No. No. No. I mean stop trying to do what you cannot do. Stop looking for security, connection, and control in what you have, who you know, or what you know. Love God and people, the way He says to love, and you will find what you really want."

"I thought I *was* loving my family. I was trying to provide."

"Do not lie to yourself. Provision is more than money."

Everett took a deep breath and gave a single nod in agreement. "So…how, exactly, do I go about 'surrendering'?" He made air quotations marks with his fingers.

"You have already begun. First, stop living in fear. Be wise, but surrender the outcome of what comes from your courage. You did this. Your life fell apart, but you did not give in to despair. You chose to hike — the hard path. You crossed the bridge. You stepped into the unknown. You conquered fear."

Everett leaned back and looked up. "Wow. You make me sound so heroic. I'm still not sure I've got fear conquered. But, okay, let's say I am conquering my fear. What then?"

"I just told you. Aim at the right things. Put what is most important in the right order. Order is the second waypoint. Seek His order. Now, get up. We must conquer the mountain."

5

THE TRAIL BEGAN A STEEP ASCENT RIGHT

out of the clearing where they had lunch. There were no trees, no grass, just rocks and a dusty trail surrounded by desolate high-mountain terrain. "We are going to 14,000 feet. The air will be thin. You must pace yourself."

"Ya. I already have a headache."

"You are dehydrated. Drink more water."

"I have been drinking."

"Not enough. More."

"Well, I also didn't sleep very well. And I don't want to have to stop to pee every few minutes. I'm in my forties. You know how that goes."

"Chh. Better to pass water than to pass out." Torgrim laughed. "That's funny! Good inspiration!" He raised his voice and shouted, "Someone put that on a coffee mug." His voice boomed, echoing off the snowcapped peaks around them. The llamas in the pasture below them took off running.

"Uhh. Ya." Everett took a few sips from the Camelback tube connected to the 3-liter container in his backpack. "Wow. I *was* dehydrated. That's already helping my head."

"Oxygen. Water gives oxygen. Americans don't drink enough water. Then you come to high mountains and die of dehydration."

The higher they hiked the more throbbing Everett felt in his head. The air was getting colder as a thick patch of grey clouds rolled in above them. "Is it normal for my lungs to burn?"

"Cold air. Altitude. Long hikes. All do strange things to your body. Even in good health altitude can crush you like an avalanche. Keeps you humble. You must stay humble in the face of the great power of nature."

"Humble. That'll get you eaten alive in my world. Every-one is out for number one. Show no weakness." He stopped and took a deep breath. "Can we stop for a second, I'm really struggling here."

"Give me your backpack. I will carry it."

Everett sat down on a boulder. "I'm fine, really."

"We are still two hours from the top and you are wobbling like a newborn elk. Give me your backpack."

Everett reluctantly handed his bag over. Torgrim hung it over his chest. He looked off into the distance. "Humility isn't weakness. Humility is knowing yourself—your strengths and weaknesses. It is honesty about who you are. It leads to meek-ness — using your strength to help the weak. It's carrying someone else's backpack when they are struggling. It's hiking slower with them, even though you could go faster."

"*Geez.* Great timing on the object lesson. You carrying my bag really makes me feel manly."

"Carry a bag now. Or carry you later. I choose the bag." He slapped Everett on the back, then took a chug from his water bottle. "Get up. We need to keep moving. Sleet is coming."

"Sleet?" He looked up at the clouds rolling in over the mountains.

"Rain plus cold equals sleet. Science, Everett, science. We need to move. Get up. I will hike behind you in case you need to be pushed."

Everett stood and began plodding up the steep path, periodically glancing at the grey clouds coming toward them. "Glad you didn't leave my rain jacket on the sidewalk in Cuzco."

"You have everything you need. And still I carry it all for you!"

A few minutes later they felt the first bits of ice begin to pelt them. Before he could ask, Torgrim handed Everett the brand-new jacket he had purchased two days before. He pulled the hood over his head and continued walking ahead. His lungs burned as he took short breaths. Every few minutes his teeth chattered uncontrollably.

The sleet got heavier and ice began forming on the trail. A thick fog descended. "I can't see where we're going, Torgrim."

"Follow the path. Every path has a destination. This is the path to where you want to go. Trust the path."

Everett shook his head. "Ya. Whatever. But it's discouraging when you can't see where you're going."

"Seen or unseen, this ancient path leads to where you want to go. Trust the path."

Everett was shivering. "This is crazy. Just an hour ago I was burning up and wanted to strip down to shorts. Now it's freezing. This temperature swing is insane."

"Nature humbles you."

"Yes. You've made that clear. Having you carry my bag also humbles me," Everett mumbled.

"Good. *Du trenger det.*"

"What?"

"Shh. Save your breath. Hike," Torgrim grunted.

Everett sighed. It was definitely a lot easier when he wasn't talking. And he couldn't imagine doing this with his backpack on. He never would have made it. He hiked in silence, struggling to take full breaths. He managed to find a consistent pace and stayed focused on each step, trying not to slip on the ice. The popping sound of the sleet hitting his jacket was peaceful in a strange way. It felt good to be in the wild, subject to the elements, with no control. Humbled.

It had been years since he had willingly taken on something that truly challenged him. He hated looking weak or foolish, though deep inside he always felt weak. So he avoided getting into situations that could humiliate him or reveal his weakness. Until he lost everything — his job, his marriage — and the humiliation was unavoidable.

"Drink." He felt something jabbing his back. He turned and Torgrim stuck the water tube from his backpack into his mouth. Everett slapped it away. "Stop. I'm not a baby that you have to feed."

"Ha! Are you sure?"

"Knock it off! Why are you obsessed with making me look like a fool? And weak…" His voice trailed off.

"Du er en stabukk."

"What?"

"You are stubborn like a goat. This is why you have stopped growing. This is why you are weak. You must be broken."

"Stopped growing? What are you talking about? I'm doing this stupid hike aren't I? This is the hardest thing I've ever done, I think."

"You are hiking. But growing? *Meh.* To grow you must embrace discomfort and be willing to look foolish and weak."

"I feel foolish and weak right now."

"Good. Then you *are* growing. Look, there. Warmiwañusca. Dead's Woman's Pass."

The clouds had cleared ahead and they could see the pass. Everett felt his eyes beginning to burn from tears. "Thank God."

"Yes. We will take a rest. Then start the dangerous part."

"Dangerous part? What was this?"

"The hard part. Injuries happen downhill, not up. When it seems easiest you are most prone to fall hardest. We will rest first."

They arrived at Dead Woman's Pass. A wooden sign noted the elevation — 4,215 meters. The wind was blowing from both sides of the pass, whipping up dust around them.

"That side of the mountain is completely clear. And the air from that direction is kind of warm. But it's still sleeting where we came from! So bizarre."

Torgrim smiled and nodded while handing Everett his backpack. "Your pack mule is retiring. You will be fine going downhill."

They sat on a rock ledge, taking in the view on both sides of the mountain. Torgrim pointed down into the green valley below in the direction they were headed next. "The flat area below the waterfall is our camp for tonight. Two more hours."

"Wow. It doesn't look that far from here."

"Steep descent. We must be cautious. *Komme.*" He stepped off a high step and began the steep descent, carefully placing each foot on the narrow Inca steps. They hiked in silence, focused on each uneven step for the next several minutes.

"I'm glad you're leading the way. If I fall I feel pretty confident you'll stop me. If I were up front and you fell…*eek*."

"Go slow. You won't fall."

"It's always so simple with you isn't it?" Everett said, sarcastically.

"Simple things take us the furthest."

"Ya…but…" He stopped himself from responding. Most of what Torgrim had been telling him *was* stuff he already knew — deep down. It really was simple. But somehow, he just hadn't been able to stick with that simplicity. He always needed to add to the simple things. But why? Was Torgrim right that fear of not getting security, connection, and control always messed up priorities? Was he afraid that the simple truths — having courage, prioritizing family and people, and not getting too big-headed — might not work?

After about two more hours of hiking, they arrived at camp just as the sun was beginning to set behind the snow-capped peaks down the valley from them. The warm air turned cold within moments of the sun disappearing. Everett grabbed his jacket out of his bag and started helping Torgrim set up the tent. "Man, these temperature fluctuations are killing me."

"I will make the tent. You pump water from the stream." He dug the filter out of his bag and handed it to Everett. "Take your headlamp. It will be very dark soon."

Everett followed the trail down to the stream and found a clearing where he could kneel down and pump the water. He looked back at the giant mountain behind them. The last rays of the sun were creating an orange glow on the snowy peaks around Dead Woman's Pass. He started pumping the water while retracing the trail they had taken coming down the mountain. *Amazing what you can do just putting one foot in front of the other.* He laughed to himself. He thought about his wife. She wouldn't believe what he was doing. His kids wouldn't either. Honestly, *he* couldn't even believe it. But he sure liked what he was feeling inside right now. He wanted to share it with his family. He thought about Torgrim's statement: *Every path has a destination.* Was there a path to getting his wife back? His family back?

Water bottles filled, he hopped back up. He could feel the pain in his knees. They had taken a quite a beating coming downhill. He looked around. It was nearly pitch black now. He flipped on his headlamp. It gave just enough light to reveal the path in front of him. He worked his way back to the camp. Torgrim had set up the tent and was boiling water on his portable burner.

They ate dinner as the temperature continued to drop. Torgrim took his last bite, looking up at the sky. "No clouds. It will freeze tonight. Bundle up."

"Well, fortunately, I'll have a personal heater in the tent with me." Everett laughed and slapped Torgrim on the back, but quickly regretted it. He pulled his hand back and tried to rub the pain out of his fingers.

"Lighthearted, Everett. Good. You are becoming much more tolerable." A subdued grin was on Torgrim's face.

"Tolerable!" Everett laughed again. "Well, I guess I'll take that as a compliment."

They climbed into the tent, zipped it up, and settled in.

JOËL MALM

6

"TODAY WILL TEST YOUR ENDURANCE. THE
longest day. But best views." Torgrim folded up the tent and
poles and shoved it into his bag.

Everett shivered while putting the last of his gear into his
backpack. "Man, it is cold when the sun isn't out."

"The sun will rise soon. Don't wear too much. The path is
very steep and you will overheat."

"But I'm freezing now."

Torgrim rolled his eyes. "Fine. Remove the jacket later."

They did one last check of the campsite, then headed out. Right out of the camp the trail was extremely steep. The narrow path hugged the side of a cliff. The higher they climbed the deeper the drop-off to their right became. Everett could feel himself getting nervous as he crossed a rickety wooden bridge barely clinging to the side of the mountain.

"Pick a point in the distance. Don't look down. Move ahead," Torgrim said in a surprisingly gently tone behind him.

Everett looked ahead and saw a round tower made of stones. "More Inca ruins?"

"Yes. Runkurakay. Short stop. Much more ahead. Are you getting hot there, Everett?"

The sun blazed over the tops of the mountains now, and with all the body heat Everett was generating climbing the hill he felt very uncomfortable in his jacket. But he was determined to act like it didn't bother him. "Nah. I'm very comfortable."

"Pfft! *Stabukk!*" Torgrim shook his head and kept plodding up the steep hill.

They arrived at the round, stone fortress of Runkurakay. Everett dropped his backpack and took off his jacket as nonchalantly as possible. He looked back at the trail they had just ascended. "Man! They didn't mess around on that trail. That was the steepest section we've had on the entire trip."

After a quick look inside the tower they stepped back onto the trail. The next section was even steeper than the first. It wasn't just steep, it was filled with boulders that required he use his hands to grip and climb. "Going up these giant rocks makes me feel like a mountain goat."

Torgrim laughed. "You are! A stubborn *stabukk*."

"That's what that means? You've been calling me a goat?"

Torgrim chuckled.

Over the next hour the only noise they exchanged was the sound of them panting for breath. Even Torgrim seemed challenged by this section. But it was strange, somehow the thoughts Everett had the previous day — the thoughts that he couldn't make it — were gone. It was like his mind had overcome some sort of block. He knew he could complete this section. They arrived at two towering boulders that looked like pillars. Walking through them they emerged at a pass in the mountains.

What Everett saw made him stop and drop his back-pack to the ground. "Holy... This is unreal," he said quietly. A seemingly endless range of snowcapped mountains jutted out of a lush green forest with wisps of white clouds hovering over the trees. Waterfalls of melting snow from the high peaks cascaded down the sides of the mountains. A magnificent Inca fortress was perched halfway down the valley on the side of a cliff.

After a few minutes of catching their breath, Torgrim stood. "We are nearly to your final waypoint on the Ancient Path." He motioned for Everett to follow him.

The trail down was extremely steep. As much as Everett wanted to look at the magnificent view around him, he had to stay focused on each step in front of him. About half an hour later they arrived at the fortress he had seen from the top of the mountain pass. A steep rock staircase that was basically a ladder led up to the fortress. It was only wide enough for one person at a time.

Torgrim smiled. "This is Sayaqmarca. Amazing place. Climb." He pointed up the staircase.

Everett began to climb, but his muscles tensed as he looked to the right. There was no railing and a fall off the side would be certain death. He looked up at the entry gate to the fortress, locked his eyes on it, then carefully worked his way up the steps.

"Good, Everett. Good," Torgrim whispered.

They arrived at the top of the stairs and stepped into the fortress. Somehow, the view was even more stunning than at the mountain pass they had just come down from.

"You have come far, friend," he said. "Here you must begin to process this experience. Experience is not the best teacher. *Evaluated* experience is. Evaluate and apply the knowledge and experience. On the trail and in life. This is wisdom — right application of knowledge. The final waypoint."

"This trip has definitely made me think more than anything in the last…well, in a long time."

"Thinking does not guarantee success. You can think your way into destruction. You thought you were fine. But woke up and realized you were not. Only wisdom guarantees success."

"That's heavy."

"Pshh," Torgrim grunted, shaking his head. "Explore the fortress. I will meet you at the entrance." He walked away, stepping behind one of the giant walls of the ruins.

Everett walked up to a chest-high wall made of giant square blocks of stone. He leaned over it. The drop-off on the other side shot a jolt of fear through him. He pulled back for a moment, looked at the giant rock, then leaned forward again. That rock was not going anywhere. He looked out at the epic scenery, sipping his water bottle. A feeling of peace came over him, like he was in a place he belonged. "This is what I want. This peace," he said to himself.

He stayed there for a few minutes, taking in the view, before he turned to explore the rest of the fortress. It was much larger than he expected, filled with stone-walled passages, lots of roofless rooms, and a giant plateau with a wall around it that gave a clear view for miles. *I could live here, if I had internet access…and a helicopter*, he thought. He turned to head back to the entrance.

Torgrim was waiting at the staircase, a contented smile on his face. "This is my favorite place. It is paradise."

They carefully worked their way back down the staircase, holding on to the wall to their right. Everett did his best to not look at the drop to his left.

The next stretch of the hike was truly a paradise filled with tropical birds, crystal clear streams running under wooden footbridges, bamboo forests, orchids, parakeets, and all sorts of tropical foliage. Lots of different Inca buildings were barely visible through the overgrown vines and ferns. "Can we stop and look at some of these ruins?" Everett yelled up ahead to Torgrim.

Torgrim stopped and turned. "Yes. But not too long. Much more ahead."

Everett stepped off the trail and went up to a large building that had been reconstructed, but was covered with moss and vines. A stream ran through an ancient aqueduct in the ruins. A flock of parakeets scattered from the trees above as he approached, their screeching becoming increasingly faint as they flew off into the valley.

In the silence of the fortress he stopped and sat on one of the cold stones. He looked at the jungle around him. It was wild and untamed. A patch of orchids grew just to his left. *What have I been doing with my life?* he thought. He had spent years running hard, trying to prove himself to the world. To himself. To his wife. To his father. He had done everything right, but the emptiness inside him had just gotten bigger. He loved his family. He really did love his wife. But he was tired of the fighting. In his marriage and in his life. He just couldn't get ahead. But this, this experience — it was like a shot of hope into his dying soul. Was this what life was about, really? Taking risks, carrying a lighter load, giving your best time and energy to family, and not always trying to prove your worth to the world? *The simple things take us the furthest.*

"*Kom igjen a!*" Torgrim's voice thundered in the distance, frightening another flock of parakeets who fluttered away.

"Coming!" Everett shouted back as he slung his backpack over his shoulder again. He popped out of the forest and back onto the trail.

Torgrim stood on the trail, smiling. They hiked through the dense greenery until they arrived at a clearing on a plateau where they ate lunch.

The trail from that point on was paved with stones, hugging the side of the mountain with no railing on the left. Certain sections of the trail were very narrow with a steep drop-off. To the right, clinging to the rock wall of the mountain was a thick orange and green moss. It gave a fairytale feel to the path. Everett gripped the moss when the trail got too narrow. He did his best to stay focused on each step, staying close to the mountain, moving ahead at a confident pace.

They came to what seemed to be an endless staircase descending into the forest. The stairs were narrow, so Everett worked his way down sideways, one step at a time. Torgrim thundered down the trail confidently. Eventually he was so far ahead that he was out of sight, leaving Everett to hike alone.

He thought about how much his two boys would love this adventure. They were always playing video games about exploring new worlds. Here he was, actually doing it. He decided he would take them on a trip like this as soon as he could afford it. What would his wife think of them going on a trip like this? The first few years of their marriage she was always proposing adventures and trips to him, but he had been so focused on building the security of his career and paying off college loans that he always shut her down. She hadn't mentioned doing a trip for years. Had she just given up on asking? A sadness came over him as he thought about what had become of their relationship — mostly because he had given his best energy to work. Was it too late to get back to what they used to have?

He rounded a corner and saw Torgrim lying on a rock, looking up at the canopy of trees above them. Torgrim looked over. "So, what will you do?"

Everett gave him a confused look as he took a sip from his Camelback. "About what?"

"About your thoughts."

"How do you know what I'm thinking about?"

"I don't. But I told you to evaluate. What is your plan?"

"*Uhm.* I guess I've been thinking that I really did have some priorities out of line. I put work and financial security over, well, pretty much everything. My wife. My kids. Of course, I was doing it for them. But somehow I lost my way."

"Yes. You did."

"I guess I'm wondering how I get back on the path if I'm so far off of it?"

"With wisdom. A journey of a thousand miles begins with one step in the right direction. Success is a direction, not a destination. Success starts the moment you begin seeking God's Kingdom."

"A direction, not a destination. I like that. Especially since I feel like I've messed things up so badly."

"God's Order restores broken things. Humble yourself. Admit your mistakes. Then take small steps in the right direction. Tomorrow, you will arrive at Machu Picchu. The city that was lost for years. You will see ruins that have been restored. Life and time broke them down. They required maintenance. They had to be rebuilt. Life is no different. Most of life is maintenance. Go home and begin to rebuild the walls of your crumbling lost city."

"Wow. That sounds so epic."

"It is." He hopped off the rock and began charging ahead. "Loving God and people is epic. Let's continue."

Everett spent the next few hours thinking about what steps he'd need to take to fix things at home. It seemed difficult, maybe impossible.

The sun was setting as they rolled into their final camp. The entire side of the mountain was covered with Inca terraces. The lowest terrace was on a cliff that dropped off into a deep valley with a roaring river, thousands of feet below them.

Torgrim pointed. "The Urumbamba River again. This is Inti Pata. Machu Picchu is just over that mountain, out of view. We camp here tonight, then to Machu Picchu tomorrow, early."

7

FOR THE FIRST TIME ON THE HIKE EVERETT

awoke before Torgrim. He lay staring at the canvas roof of the tent, listening to the rumble of the river below them. The peace was interrupted at intervals by the roar of Torgrim's snoring. Everett poked at the giant, hoping to wake him. He wouldn't move, so Everett stepped out of the tent.

A faint orange glow hovered over the white mountain range in front of him. A sliver of the moon hung low in the sky. He heard the horn of a train and looked into the valley. A single light was winding its way through the valley, right along the river.

"That is your ride home," Torgrim said from behind him in his gravely morning voice.

"Wow. Way down there. I don't think this trip would have been the same if I had taken the train." He bit his lip. "Torgrim, thank you. Really, thank you."

Torgrim smiled. "I only made the offer. You made the choice. But, you are welcome."

They packed up camp as the sun slowly worked its way above the mountains.

"Final section of the trail. Let's go." Torgrim took a deep breath, scanned the horizon, then began descending the steps next to the terraces and back onto the trail. At the bottom of the stairs Torgrim had Everett take lead. A few minutes into the hike they came to a fork in the trail. "Which way?" Everett asked.

"You go left. I'm going right."

Everett felt his heart begin to race. "What?"

"I leave you here, friend." Torgrim flung his backpack around to his chest, stuck his hand in his pack, and pulled out a black, hard-covered journal. "Take this. In Machu Picchu, write what you have learned — the four waypoints. Courage, Order, Humility, Wisdom. Rebuild your lost city on those truths. Make it strong so your house — your life — will not crumble in difficult times. Then teach others to do the same. I must go."

"Wait, you can't leave. I don't know where I'm going. What if I get lost?"

"Follow the Ancient Path. It will still guide you now. I must go. I have a train to catch."

"Wait, you're taking the train back?"

Torgrim laughed. "Of course, as will you."

"Can we meet up in Cuzco?"

"I will be gone when you return. Now, go."

"Wait!"

Torgrim turned, smiled, gave a sharp salute with his right hand, then turned back around and walked away.

As his Nordic guardian angel disappeared into the foliage, Everett felt a deep sadness come over him. He heard a distant rumble of thunder over the mountains to his left. He looked back and forth at the two paths. He was tempted to follow Torgrim, but he hadn't come this far to not see Machu Picchu. And he didn't want to incur Torgrim's wrath for following him. He took a deep breath, then took the left fork in the road toward Machu Picchu.

An hour later he climbed a series of Inca stairs with a sign at the top that announced he had arrived. INTI PUNKU, The Sun Gate. He rounded a stone column and deep in the green, misty valley ahead of him he saw it — the ancient lost city of Machu Picchu. He was still high above it, but it was unmistakable.

The sadness he felt from being left by Torgrim was replaced with a sense of relief and calm. He began walking down the final stretch of the trail that snaked its way along the side of the mountain and into Machu Picchu. The closer he got to the lost city, the more magnificent it became.

What must it have been like at the peak of its power? Those who built it must have never imagined that one day it would be abandoned and turn to rubble. Forgotten for centuries. Rediscovered. And rebuilt.

The entire complex, rebuilt with the same ancient stones. It gave him a sense of hope for his own project — rebuilding his family and life. He walked to the far end of the site. He found a shade tree and sat down, leaning his back against a giant limestone boulder. He pulled out the notebook Torgrim had given him and began writing, giving a full page to each waypoint he had learned:

1
Courage

I will not ignore my fears or make decisions based on them.

I will face what I fear in small doses.

Fear will not go away, but I will do it afraid.

Fear will lose its hold on me.

2
Order

I have limited resources of time, money, and energy.

Something must always be sacrificed to give
my best to what matters most.

I will give my best resources to my wife, my kids,
people I love, and then everything else.

3
Humility

I will have an accurate view of what I am
and what I am not.

I will welcome challenges that require me to learn new things.

I will stay humble and listen carefully
to advice and guidance.

4
Wisdom

I will choose to trust in God and
not lean on my ideas or thoughts.

I will seek His Order — His Kingdom —
and what He wants from me.

Then I will do those things.

He closed the notebook and looked out over the vast fortress. Groups of tourists were scattered around the site. It was strange being back around people after so many days away. He explored the ruins and climbed to the highest point of the complex. Then he headed to the entrance and boarded a bus back down the mountain. Sitting in the soft seat of the bus, with air-conditioning, felt indulgent after what he had just been through.

A clean-shaven man in perfectly pressed, clean outdoorsman clothes walked down the aisle and stopped to take a seat. He saw Everett and gave a concerned look.

Everett offered a smile. "Sorry, I'm a little dirty. I haven't had a shower in days."

The man cautiously sat down next to him. "Did you hike in?"

He put his shoulders back and took a deep breath. "Yes."

The man raised his eyebrows. "Wow. Impressive. You are much more adventurous than me."

"Probably not." He chuckled. "Just didn't know what I was doing. But I'm glad I did it."

The bumpy dirt road into the valley was one switchback after another. The driver made some pretty harrowing turns with the giant bus. But Everett was too tired to be concerned. He leaned his head back on the headrest and dozed off. He awoke to the bus pulling into the bustling village of Aguas Calientes. The river that was so far below him on the hike was now churning right next to him as he stepped off the bus.

He made a beeline for a pizza restaurant. After lunch, he found a hotel that allowed him to take a shower for a few soles. He went to the train station and purchased a return ticket to Cuzco, departing later that afternoon. Then he went to the market and purchased some souvenirs to give to his boys. He also bought a soft, white alpaca blanket for his wife.

The train ride back to Cuzco was slow and uneventful. He was able to retrace many of his steps in reverse as the train rumbled past places he had seen looking down from the mountain peaks high above.

It was dark by the time the train arrived in Poroy, the village just outside of Cuzco where the trains stopped. A bus picked him up and took him back to his hotel.

His entire body was aching. He took a warm shower, then fell asleep quickly and slept hard the entire night.

The following morning he headed back to the restaurant he had visited when he first arrived. The young man who had served him a few days earlier greeted him. "Hola, señor, how was *el camino* to Machu Picchu?"

"Uhm. The hike was, well…life changing."

The young man grinned. "Yes. Many people say this." He pointed toward the patio overlooking the square. "Do you want the same table as last time?"

The young man led Everett to the patio. He sat down and looked out over the square. The waiter placed a menu in front of him then turned to walk away.

"Hey, do you know how to get ahold of Torgrim?" Everett asked.

"Torgrim?" The boy turned, a confused look on his face.

"Ya, the big guy who was in here. He came to my table. The one who took me on the hike."

The boy cocked his head. "Big guy?"

"Ya. The huge Norwegian guy with the long, blonde, braided hair."

"Uhm. I don't know what you are talking about."

Everett was getting frustrated. "The huge guy I was talking with last time."

"Señor, you were alone last time."

"I know. But then Torgrim came to my table. He bought me a beer."

The boy shrugged. "I don't know who you are talking about.

Epilogue

JOËL MALM

Epilogue

EVERETT FINISHED THE DISHES AND WALKED
into the dining room. He smiled at his sons who were finishing their homework at the kitchen table. In the living room his wife was reading an article on a digital tablet. He walked over and kissed her head, then sat down next to her. She smiled and squeezed his hand.

"Whatcha reading there?" he asked.

"Crazy story. There was a huge fire at this apartment complex in Chile and some hero rescued all these people. Some giant man. Pretty amazing. They described him as being like some Norwegian god."

"Norwegian god?" He looked over at the screen. His eyes widened when he saw the picture. It was Torgrim emerging from a burning building with four children thrown over his shoulders.

He laughed. Then he leaned back and smiled.

Check out
more from
Joël

Adventure and Coaching | *SummitLeaders.com*

the **malm**
podcast

Anger. Anxiety. Frustration. Worry. We've all felt the power of these emotions, and lived to regret the speed with which we spoke from, or even acted on them.

We know we need to slow down and calm down before that torrent of emotion sweeps us away—but how?

What if you could understand those feelings better? Not ignore them or stuff them down, but actually harness their power to improve your relationships?

That's the journey Joël will take you on in *Love Slows Down*. Whether you're feeling the constant weight of worry, flashes of fury, or the exhaustion of always being on edge, there is a way to understand what triggers your emotions and put the brakes on. You can slow down and respond with love.

A few years back, Joël had the idea to lead people on outdoor expeditions around the world with a spiritual focus. He started what is now Summit Leaders.

This book is a response to the question he often gets: How do you do something like that?

Whether you want to start a business, raise a family, run a marathon, plant a church, restore a relationship, or climb a mountain, you can take practical steps to see your vision come to be.

Vision Map is not a formula for overnight success, but it is a template to start anyone on the path to envisioning a God-given dream. God often gives us a difficult problem to solve, and we just need a push in the right direction to find the answer.

Choose What to Lose

A traveler is happier the lighter his load.
—*Marcus Felix*

Most of the people who go on expeditions with me have never done a major hike before. Which is what I want. I'm not looking for people who are all wildernessy and willing to chop off their arm with a Swiss Army knife to survive. Those people would be really out of place on my teams. (Plus, I don't want them around—they'll make me look like a wimp!)

Because the people in my groups are all first-timers, they're usually really concerned about having the correct gear. I get tons of texts and emails asking exactly what they should bring. So before our trips, I give them a packing list and have them watch a video I recorded about how to pack for a hike. I show them exactly what I bring. I want them to feel confident without over-packing, but most team members still bring way too much with them. (Some commission-based salesperson at the outdoor store probably saw them coming and convinced them they needed every gadget possible or they would die on a mountain.) They show up for the hike loaded down with gear.

This is a serious problem.

A pack that's too heavy will wear you out, and you won't be able to successfully complete the hike. So the night before we leave for the trail, I'll often do a gear weigh-in. I set a weight goal for their bags. If it's too heavy, I have them start pulling stuff out of it.

This process gets highly emotional in a hurry. People get really sensitive about their stuff. I've seen grown men—CEOs of large organizations—nearly in tears when I have them leave some things behind. Some folks even get angry. One girl who I wouldn't let bring a hairdryer (on a trail that had no electricity!) was mad at me for days. As I lighten their loads, I can see the fear in their eyes— but I know they'll get over it. Usually by the second day of the hike, those same people thank me for making them lighten their loads. They realize just how hard the hike would have been with all that extra weight.

I'm convinced that nobody intends to overpack. It happens slowly, little by little. We're afraid of not having something we may need, so we just take everything. It's wise to prepare, but you can't prepare for everything. We end up overloaded and tired. By the way, I'm not talking about packing for a trip anymore. I'm talking about life.

Life is like a long hike, and most of us are walking along with a pack that is way too heavy. We're all doing our best to provide for our families and give them the opportunities we never had. We figure if we can just get a little more, we'll have everything we need. But slowly, little by little, we get overloaded.

Our finances are overloaded. We spend everything we make, or more.

Our time is overloaded. Work deadlines, overtime, kids' sports schedules.

Our energy is overloaded. I heard someone say, "The world is run by tired people." Basically, yes.

Like a hiker picking up rocks along the trail, thinking we might need them at some point to throw at a bear or lion, we take on more and more. A lot of what we add to our load is actually good stuff—opportunities, relationships. But as the weight builds, we feel overwhelmed, like we're carrying around a giant pack. We're strong. But not that strong. We end up tired and dread every day, saying, "Again? I'm tired and I can't carry all this anymore."

At some point, we have to slow down (maybe even stop) and really look at what we're bringing with us. We have to figure out if all the stuff we're carrying is helping us or hindering us in getting to where we want to be. At some point, we have to decide to leave a few things behind.

Love slows down to choose what to lose.

Define the Destination

We all have an idea in mind of what the good life looks like. We have a destination in mind. Sometimes we get those ideas from how we were raised. Other times we get them from other people telling us what we should want—what makes for the good life. We may never write it down or say it out loud, but we all have a picture of what having security, connection, and control looks like—a nice home, a loving marriage, kids who go further than we ever did in education or work. It's good to have a goal. You need something to aim at. King Solomon said, "Where there is no prophetic vision the people cast off restraint." A prophetic vision is just a mental picture of where you want to go. If you don't know where you're going, it's really easy to "cast off restraint" and just take everything—even things you don't really need.

When you know where you want to go, you'll know what to pack. And what not to pack. You don't pack flip-flops to climb through the snows of Mount Kilimanjaro. You don't take a warm goose-down parka for hiking through the Amazon. Life is no different. When you know where you want to go, it's a lot easier to know what to bring with you and what needs to be left behind.

When we've decided where we want to go in life, we start packing accordingly. We fill our lives with whatever promises to get us the security, connection, or control we want for our families and ourselves. Anything that you believe will get you where you want to go has value to you. But if we aren't careful, we can add so much to our lives that we actually start to weigh ourselves down. Rather than improve our chances of getting us to our destinations, without realizing it, we can actually hinder our abilities in the long run. So to do a good gear check for your life, you need to start by looking at what you value.

A Question of Values

I hear this line a lot: "I really want to travel more, but it's so expensive. How can you afford to travel so much?" They look at my beat-up fifteen-year-old car, and it's pretty clear that I'm not rolling in money. And they are correct. But that old car is a big part of the reason I can afford to travel so much.

Having a nice, new car isn't that important to me. But travel is. So rather than making a car payment every month, I take what would have been spent on the payment and divide it up into savings—a little for travel and a little for when we'll need a new (older) car. Emily and I both value travel, so we decided to live in a house that is worth way less than what we can afford. When we travel, we do it cheaply. We travel with friends and split costs. In fact, we can do a two-week trip to Europe for what most people spend on four months of car payments. We value travel more than having a new car, so we do whatever it takes to scrimp and save to do it. There is absolutely nothing wrong with having a nice, dependable vehicle. (Honestly, sometimes we do get a little jealous of people with nice, shiny cars with no dents in them.) There's nothing wrong with having a big, beautiful, expensive home. It's just that travel is more important to us than those things. So we put our money, time, and energy toward travel.

We all have certain things that we value—travel, a nice home, a secure job, loving relationships, respect. Values are unique to each person, and there are an unlimited number of things you can value. Some of our values are learned through how we were raised. Some are just adopted—without much question—based on the society or culture we live in. And the truth is, many of our values come from doing whatever it takes to make sure the thing we fear the most doesn't come upon us. We may not be sure exactly what we want, but we know what we don't want. And we run as fast as we can away from those things. When we live in fear, we tend to value whatever will remove the fear that threatens us.

We naturally give our time, money, and energy to those things that we believe will get us where we want to go or keep us away from what we fear the most. That's part of what Jesus was talking about when He said, "Where your treasure is, there will your heart be also." If you want to know what your heart is set on, look at where you spend your time, money, and energy (your treasures). In other words: Our actions always show what we truly value. If you want to know what you really value, look at what you do—not what you say or think or feel.

If you work a lot of hours, then work and financial security are probably values for you.

If you engage in all sorts of online debates and always want the latest gossip, then drama has a high value for you.

If you exercise a lot, health or how you look is of high value.

What we do makes it clear what we really value. We naturally give our time, money, and energy to what we truly value most.

I drive an old car. Now I would love to travel and also be able to drive a new car, but my bank account tells me that's just not possible. I've only got so much income and so much money. And this is the challenge we all eventually face.

We are limited.

We only have so much time, money, and energy. Because we're limited, we're forced to figure out what is truly of highest value at some point. Not every value can have equal value. If everything has the same value, nothing has value. You can be certain that if you are trying to give everything equal value, you'll experience lots of anger and anxiety. You'll also get really tired.

There needs to be a hierarchy to our values. Some things have to be more important than others. And sometimes things that are of lesser importance will have to be pulled out of our pack and left behind. Sometimes we have to sacrifice good things to give our best to the best things.

The Right Sacrifice

The first time we read about anger in the Bible is also the first time we read about sacrifice. Cain and his brother Abel bring an offering—a sacrifice—to God. For some reason, God rejects Cain's offering.

Cain gets angry.

God asks him, "Why are you angry, and why has your face fallen? If you do well, will you not be accepted? And if you do not do well, sin is crouching at the door. Its desire is contrary to you, but you must rule over it."

The word translated "sin" (chata) in this verse comes from an archery term that means "to miss the mark." God basically tells Cain that he aimed wrong. He missed it. He had the wrong goal. God didn't value what Cain valued, so his sacrifice didn't count.

There are wrong sacrifices.

I talk to people all the time who realized too late that they sacrificed their marriage for their career. Hospitals are filled with people who sacrificed their health for the sake of pleasure and convenience. Lots of people sacrifice their long-term relationship with their kids, all in the name of providing financial security for them. They spend hours away from their families to provide them with money, but what the family really wants is their presence.

Here's the really hard pill to swallow: You can live a morally upright life—be faithful to your wife, pay your taxes, provide for your family. But if you value the wrong things, you can end up feeling the same negative results as actual sin—remorse and regret.

A pastor recently shared with me that he was angry and resented his wife for leaving him. He humbly bragged about how he had been faithful to her, prayed for her, and loved her. He made lots of sacrifices to be in the ministry. He was angry at his spouse and kids for not being supportive of the "call" on his life. But his wife was angry too. She said he put ministry to others ahead of caring for his own family. After some soul-searching, he admitted that he had sacrificed his family for the affirmation he got from always being available to his church. He made a lot of sacrifices for ministry, but he sacrificed the wrong things. It's possible to be very sincere and loyal to those you love but still make the wrong sacrifice. You can aim wrong. You have to keep a constant eye on what is really being sacrificed. What makes this even more challenging is the fact that values are a moving target. In the next chapter, we'll see that some values shouldn't change, but lots of them have to be adjusted based on what season of life you're in. When seasons change—you get married, have kids, change jobs, make transitions, kids leave the house—you will need to make some changes to your value structure. If you are still doggedly pursuing goals that you set for yourself in your teens, twenties, or thirties without making adjustments for new values that have appeared since then—like kids and a spouse—there's a good chance some of your values that arrived more recently on the scene may be suffering because of it. Some values should change with new seasons.

So how do you know if a value needs to change? Great question. Fortunately, there's a pretty simple sign that your values may need to be adjusted. You just have to go back and visit with your friendly personal consultant. Anger or frustration in yourself or those around you is a good sign that some values might need adjustment. It's a sign that you may need to change some priorities to make sure you're only carrying what you need for this phase of your journey.

Get honest about where you are in life. Is there an issue that is constantly a point of contention in your home or work? Is there something that is always igniting anger in you or those around you? Is it possible that something you truly value is unintentionally getting less time, energy, or money than it deserves? What do your actions show that you really value? I'd encourage you to take some time to compare what you say you value and what your actions say you value. If you've never thought through what you really value, consider writing it out. Often just taking the time to slow down and define what you really value—writing it down—can help relieve the tension.

After looking at your life and evaluating what you're carrying, you may decide you need to leave a few things behind. Letting some things go isn't failure. It's actually success. It may be hard, but I'm pretty sure you won't regret lightening your load. A traveler is happier the lighter his or her load is. Which is why it's so important to get really clear about where you want to go and what you value. Something always has to be sacrificed to make room for what's most important. Knowing exactly what to sacrifice means you need to prioritize.

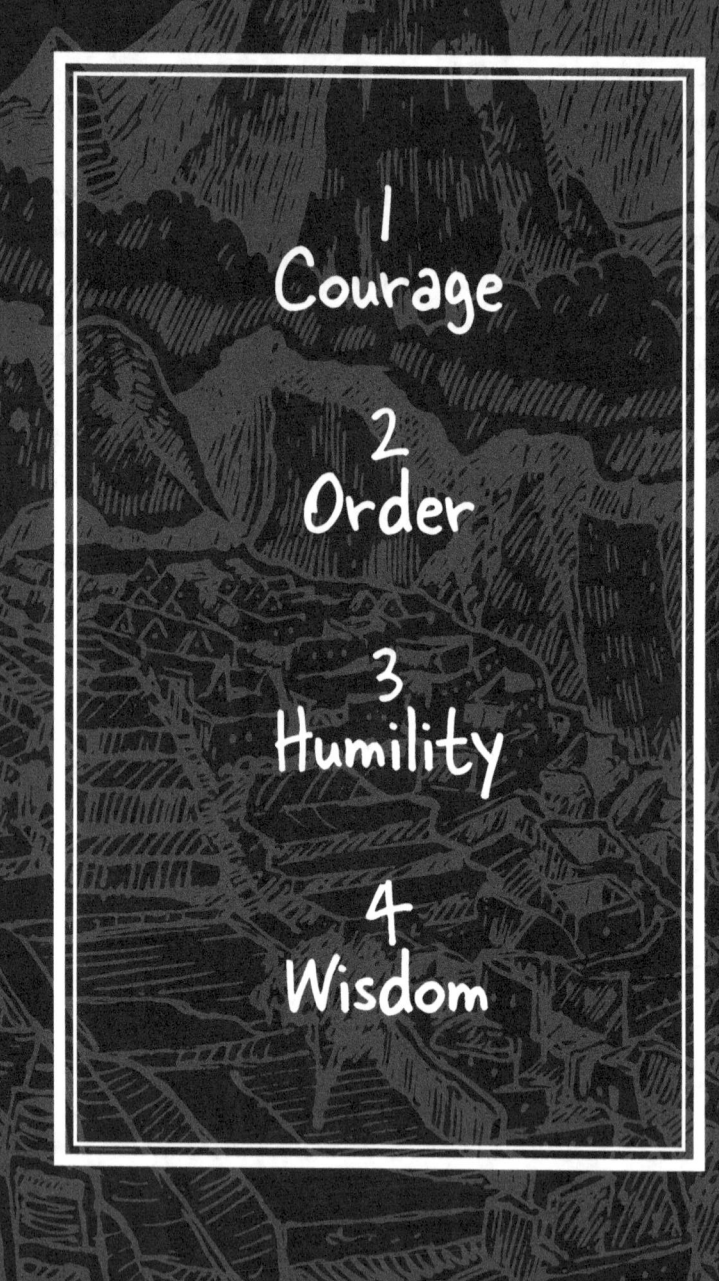

1
Courage

2
Order

3
Humility

4
Wisdom